THE GRAPHIC NOVELS SERIES

WUTHERING HEIGHTS

EMILY BRONTË

RETOLD BY HILARY BURNINGHAM
ILLUSTRATED BY TRACY FENNELL

Evans

EVANS BROTHERS LIMITED

Published by
Evans Brothers Limited
2A Portman Mansions
Chiltern Street
London W1U 6NR

© in the modern text Hilary Burningham 2004
© in the illustrations Evans Brothers Ltd 2004
Designed by Design Systems Ltd

British Library Cataloguing in Publication Data
Burningham, Hilary
Wuthering Heights – (The graphic novels series)
1. Yorkshire (England) – Social life and customs – 19th century – Juvenile fiction
2. Children's stories
I. Title
II. Brontë, Emily, 1818–1848. Wuthering Heights 823.9'14(J)
ISBN 0237 52581X

Printed in Malta by Gutenberg Press

GENEALOGICAL TABLE

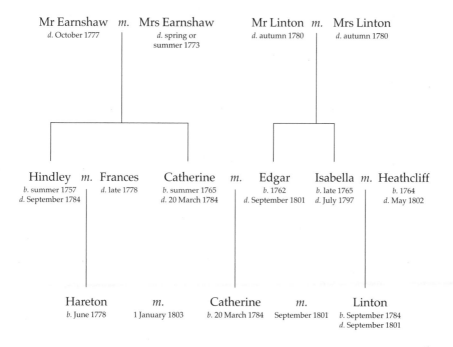

Mr Earnshaw	*m.*	Mrs Earnshaw		Mr Linton	*m.*	Mrs Linton
d. October 1777		*d.* spring or summer 1773		*d.* autumn 1780		*d.* autumn 1780

Hindley	*m.*	Frances	Catherine	*m.*	Edgar	Isabella	*m.*	Heathcliff
b. summer 1757		*d.* late 1778	*b.* summer 1765		*b.* 1762	*b.* late 1765		*b.* 1764
d. September 1784			*d.* 20 March 1784		*d.* September 1801	*d.* July 1797		*d.* May 1802

Hareton	*m.*	Catherine	*m.*	Linton
b. June 1778	1 January 1803	*b.* 20 March 1784	September 1801	*b.* September 1784
				d. September 1801

Volume One

My name is Lockwood and I have rented a place called Thrushcross Grange, in Yorkshire. It is owned by a Mr Heathcliff, who lives four miles away in a house called Wuthering[1] Heights. Earlier today, I went there to meet him. He was very unfriendly, glowering at me from under thick, black eyebrows. His servant, Joseph, was an old, old man, who also glared at me.

The front door of the house opened straight into a large sitting room. Under a large dresser was a female dog, surrounded by puppies. Other dogs lurked around the room.

Heathcliff went down to the cellar. Left alone, I pulled faces at the female dog. I should have known better. She attacked me, as did the other dogs. I shouted for help and to my relief a woman rushed in from the kitchen waving a frying pan. She calmed the dogs and left.

Heathcliff and I talked over a glass of wine. He was an intelligent man. On leaving I said I would return the next day. He did not seem to wish another visit, but I was determined to come back, nevertheless.

---

[1] 'wuthering' is a Yorkshire word meaning the sound the wind makes when it is blowing or blustery

'Mr Lockwood, your new tenant, sir – I do myself the honour of calling as soon as possible, after my arrival, to express the hope that I have not inconvenienced you by my perseverance in soliciting the occupation of Thrushcross Grange...'

(Mr Lockwood to Mr Heathcliff, Volume I, Chapter I)

The next day, I returned to Wuthering Heights.
As I arrived, it was starting to snow. A young man
carrying a pitchfork led me to the sitting room,
where a table was laid with plenty of food.

This time, a young woman, whom I took to be Mrs
Heathcliff, was in the room. She seemed no more
friendly than her husband. She was very scornful,
especially when I mistook a heap of dead rabbits for
pet cats. The young man who had shown me in stood
before the fire and glared at me. I could not tell
whether he was servant or family.

When Heathcliff came in, he spoke rudely to the
young woman. We all sat down to tea. It turned out
that the woman was Heathcliff's daughter-in-law.
Her husband, Heathcliff's son, was dead. The young
man was Hareton Earnshaw, the same as the name
written in the stonework at the front of the house.
The fire burned brightly and the food was good, but
the atmosphere was very unpleasant.

Meanwhile, the snow had continued falling. I had no
idea how to get back to Thrushcross Grange. It was
decided that I would stay the night. Zillah, the cook,
showed me upstairs.

'Ah, your favourites are among these!' I continued, turning
to an obscure cushion full of something like cats.
'A strange choice of favourites,' she observed scornfully.
Unluckily, it was a heap of dead rabbits...

(Lockwood to Catherine, Volume I, Chapter II)

Zillah told me that the master did not usually allow people to stay in the room where he had told her to take me. Instead of a bed, there was a large oak case built around the window with an old-fashioned couch inside. It was like a small room or closet, with sliding panels. I climbed inside. It felt safe.

That night I had terrible nightmares. I heard a branch tapping against the window. In trying to open it to stop the noise, I broke the pane. To my horror, I felt the fingers of a small, icy hand. A voice begged, 'Let me in – let me in!' and a child's face appeared at the window. I piled some books against the window, but I could still hear the wailing voice outside. I shouted at it to go away.

My shouts brought Heathcliff, furious at being disturbed. He sent me out of the room, but I heard him throw open the window, sobbing and begging the ghost to come in. I could not understand why Heathcliff seemed to think it real. It had been part of my nightmares.

I decided never again to visit Wuthering Heights. In the morning, I left as soon as I could.

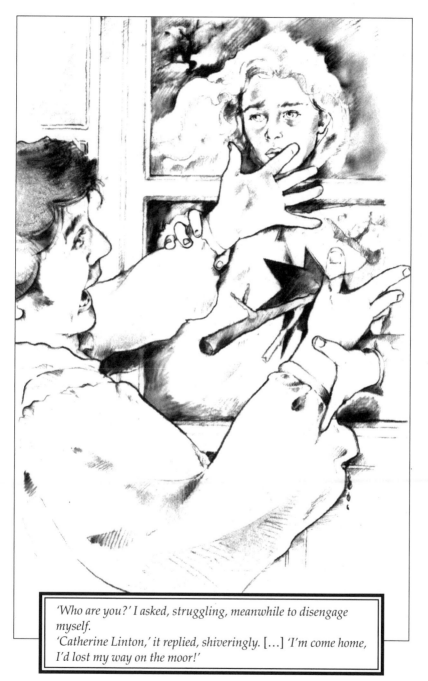

'Who are you?' I asked, struggling, meanwhile to disengage myself.
'Catherine Linton,' it replied, shiveringly. [...] 'I'm come home, I'd lost my way on the moor!'

(Lockwood to the ghostly child, Volume I, Chapter III)

I had rented Thrushcross Grange to keep away from people, but I found myself feeling lonely and bored. I invited my housekeeper, Mrs Ellen[1] Dean, to sit with me while I ate supper. I asked her about the family at Wuthering Heights. Here is Mrs Dean's story…

*****

Before coming to Thrushcross Grange, I[2] was at Wuthering Heights. My mother was the nurse to Mr Hindley Earnshaw, Hareton's father. As a child I was the friend of Hindley and his sister, Miss Cathy, who was then only six years old.

One day, old Mr Earnshaw returned from the market with a dirty, ragged, black-haired boy. He had found the child in Liverpool, starving, with nowhere to go. The boy was called Heathcliff. From the beginning, he caused trouble. Hindley was jealous and sometimes bullied the boy. Mr Earnshaw punished Hindley if he found out.

Heathcliff was a strange child. He didn't show any gratitude to Mr Earnshaw for rescuing him from the streets, but he didn't make a fuss about Hindley's bullying, either. I thought he didn't mind, but I was wrong, completely wrong.

[1] the short form of Ellen is Nelly – Ellen Dean is usually referred to as 'Nelly' in the story
[2] Nelly takes up the story from this point, in her own words

I had a peep at a dirty, ragged, black-haired child; big enough
both to walk and talk – indeed, its face looked older than
Catherine's – yet, when it was set on its feet, it only stared
round, and repeated over and over again some gibberish that
nobody could understand.

(Nelly Dean, describing the arrival of Heathcliff, Volume I, Chapter IV)

Hindley resented Heathcliff. Mr Earnshaw tried to protect him from Hindley, but he was getting old. Finally Hindley was sent away to school.

Left to ourselves, we would all have got on quite well, except for Miss Cathy and old Joseph, the servant. Joseph was very religious, while Miss Cathy was always up to mischief. Sometimes she slapped people and ordered them about. I would not be treated that way, and told her so.

Cathy cared a great deal for Heathcliff. Her worst punishment was to be separated from him. She loved her father, too, but teased him as she did everyone else.

One night, as he slept in his chair with Cathy and Heathcliff at his feet, Mr Earnshaw died. Joseph realised he was dead and tried to get Cathy and Heathcliff to go to bed. When Cathy hugged her father goodnight, she realised he was dead.

Joseph sent me to get the doctor and the parson[1]. On the way back, I looked in on Cathy and Heathcliff. They were talking together about Mr Earnshaw being in heaven. I wished we were all in heaven together … safe.

[1]parson – vicar

'I shall bid father good night first,' said Catherine, putting her arms round his neck, before we could hinder her.
'Oh, he's dead, Heathcliff, he's dead!'.
And they both set up a heart-breaking cry.

(Volume I, Chapter V)

Mr Hindley came home for Mr Earnshaw's funeral, and brought with him – a wife! She seemed very happy, though young and thin, with a bad cough. Mr Hindley, who had been away for four years, was now master of the house. He stopped Heathcliff's education and made him work as a labourer.

One Sunday, Catherine and Heathcliff disappeared. Late that night, Heathcliff returned without her and told me about their adventure. They had gone over the moors to spy on the Lintons, the family who at that time lived at Thrushcross Grange. Peering in through the drawing room windows, they saw a luxurious room with two children having a quarrel over a little dog. Catherine and Heathcliff thought it ridiculous to behave in this way, and laughed aloud.

On hearing their laughter, the Lintons had them brought into the house. The boy, Edgar, had seen Catherine at church and she was welcomed. But the Lintons were horrified by Heathcliff's wild appearance and bad language. He was sent home. Through the window, he saw Catherine being admired and spoiled.

I told him to go to bed. I was certain that he would be punished. Sure enough, Hindley told him never to speak to Miss Catherine again or he would be sent away for ever.

'Afterwards, they dried and combed her beautiful hair, and gave her a pair of enormous slippers, and wheeled her to the fire [...] I saw they were full of stupid admiration; she is so immeasurably superior to them — to everybody on Earth, is she not, Nelly?'

(Heathcliff, talking to Nelly, Volume I, Chapter VI)

Wuthering Heights

Cathy stayed five weeks at Thrushcross Grange. On
Christmas Eve she returned, elegant and grown-up.

On Christmas Day Heathcliff asked me to help him
be good. He envied Edgar Linton's light hair and fair
skin. I told Heathcliff that he was handsome in a
different way. His parents could have been foreign
kings or queens. He was comforted and began to
look quite pleasant.

The Earnshaws returned from church with the
Lintons. Edgar Linton was rude about Heathcliff's
freshly-combed hair. This was all too much for
Heathcliff. He grabbed a dish of hot apple-sauce and
flung it into Edgar's face. Hindley gave Heathcliff a
beating and locked him in his room.

All day, Heathcliff was alone. Catherine was very
upset. Later I let him come downstairs and sit by the
fire, where I offered him some of the Christmas feast.
But Heathcliff did not want food. He was planning
how to pay back Hindley. I became worried. Revenge
was only for God.

*****

Mrs Dean paused, feeling that she had talked for too
long. I[1], however, begged her to continue, without
missing any details.

*****

[1] Lockwood

He seized a tureen of hot apple-sauce, the first thing that came under his gripe [grasp], and dashed it full against the speaker's face and neck – who instantly commenced a lament that brought Isabella and Catherine hurrying to the place.

(Volume I, Chapter VII)

Mrs Dean continued …

Twenty-three years ago, in 1778, Frances Earnshaw, Hindley's wife, had a beautiful baby boy. Sadly, Frances was ill and died soon afterwards.

I took charge of the baby, whose name was Hareton. Mr Hindley drowned his sorrows by drinking. He mistreated everyone, especially Heathcliff. Joseph and I were the only servants left. Only Edgar Linton came to the house sometimes to visit Miss Cathy.

Miss Cathy, now aged fifteen, was the most beautiful girl in the neighbourhood. She was determined and selfish, but to the Lintons she showed only her good side. They all loved her, especially Edgar. But they despised Heathcliff. Cathy remained loyal to him, though she never showed it to the Lintons.

One afternoon, Edgar came to visit Cathy. She had a tantrum because I refused to leave them alone together. Mr Hindley had told me not to. Cathy slapped me. She slapped Edgar. Edgar said he was leaving, but Cathy threatened to cry until she made herself sick. Edgar stayed, and by the time Mr Hindley returned, drunk, they had decided they were in love.

She stamped her foot, wavered a moment, and then irresistibly impelled by the naughty spirit within her, slapped me on the cheek a stinging blow that filled both eyes with water.
'Catherine, love! Catherine!' interposed Linton, greatly shocked at the double fault of falsehood and violence which his idol had committed.

(Volume I, Chapter VIII)

When Hindley came home drunk he often became violent. Once, Hindley found Hareton and held him, kicking and screaming, over the bannister. Hareton squirmed out of his arms and fell down into the hall. At that moment, Heathcliff happened to walk underneath and caught the toddler. From his face, it was clear that he wished he hadn't. What a wonderful revenge if he had allowed Hareton to be killed by his own father!

Later, Cathy came into the kitchen where I sat rocking Hareton to tell me that Edgar Linton had asked her to marry him – and she had accepted. She said that Edgar was good looking. He would be rich, and she would be the most important woman in the neighbourhood. I told her that these were not good reasons for getting married. Cathy admitted that she really wanted to marry Heathcliff, but Hindley had brought him so low that she could not consider it. She could never let him know how much she loved him, even though she felt that they were part of each other.

I suddenly realised that Heathcliff was in the room. When he heard Cathy say that she could never marry him, he quietly left. He didn't hear her declare how much she loved him.

There was scarcely time to experience a thrill of horror before we saw that the little wretch was safe. Heathcliff arrived underneath just at the critical moment; by a natural impulse, he arrested his descent, and setting him on his feet, looked up to discover the author of the accident.

(Volume I, Chapter IX)

Next, Cathy told me that she intended to use her power and money, as Linton's wife, to help Heathcliff. Heathcliff, she said, gave her life meaning. I suddenly lost patience with her. She seemed to have no idea of what she was saying.

That night, Heathcliff could not be found. Cathy kept looking for him and got soaking wet in the rain. When she came in, she refused to change her clothes. By morning, she was ill. She grieved for Heathcliff with terrible weeping. I thought she was going mad.

Later, the Lintons took Cathy to Thrushcross Grange. Sadly, old Mrs Linton and her husband caught the fever. They died a few days later.

When Cathy returned home, she was even more badly behaved, having constant tantrums. The doctor said she should have her own way, but this made her worse. She was rude to everyone.

Edgar was still in love with her, and three years later they were married. They asked me to go to Thrushcross Grange with them. I hated to leave little Hareton, who was then nearly five. But Edgar offered me good wages and Hindley ordered me out of the house. I had no choice …

*****

'Nelly, I am Heathcliff – he's always, always in my mind – not as a pleasure, any more than I am always a pleasure to myself – but, as my own being – so, don't talk of our separation again – it is impracticable; and — '

(Cathy to Nelly Dean, Volume I, Chapter IX)

I, Lockwood, had four weeks of illness. Dr Kenneth said I would probably not leave the house before the spring. I asked Mrs Dean to come and finish her story. Mr Heathcliff had run off and not been heard of for three years. Miss Cathy had married Edgar Linton. I wanted to know what happened next. Mrs Dean took up her story again …

*****

Miss Catherine and I[1] went to Thrushcross Grange. For six months she was on her best behaviour. Edgar made sure that no one upset her.

One evening, as I was going into the house, I met – Heathcliff! He insisted on speaking to Catherine. She went down to speak to him. I told Edgar that Heathcliff had returned. He insisted that Cathy bring him inside.

Heathcliff was completely changed. He was now a well-formed, athletic man. His manner was dignified and his face intelligent. He and Catherine were delighted to see each other.

Edgar, Catherine, Isabella (Edgar's sister) and Heathcliff all sat down to tea. Heathcliff soon left. Hindley Earnshaw, he said, had invited him to stay at Wuthering Heights.

[1] Nelly is speaking from this point

'I shall think it a dream tomorrow!' she cried. 'I shall not be able to believe that I have seen, and touched, and spoken to you once more – and yet, cruel Heathcliff, you don't deserve this welcome. To be absent and silent for three years, and never to think of me!'

(Volume I, Chapter X)

That night, I was uneasy. Why had Heathcliff returned? He was paying good rent to Hindley Earnshaw in return for staying at Wuthering Heights. Hindley needed the money to pay for his gambling and drinking.

Heathcliff came often to Thrushcross Grange. Isabella Linton was then eighteen years old. To Edgar's horror, his sister began to be attracted to Heathcliff. Catherine tried to convince her that he was an evil person who would marry her for the Linton money. I told her what old Joseph had told me: that Hindley and Heathcliff drank and gambled day and night. Isabella refused to believe it, but I knew that it was the truth.

The next day, Heathcliff called while Mr Edgar was in town. Catherine began to play a cruel game. She told Heathcliff that she and Isabella both loved him. Isabella was horribly embarrassed and begged Cathy to stop. Heathcliff became quiet and thoughtful.

When Isabella left the room, he asked if Cathy had been speaking the truth. Then he asked if Isabella was Edgar's heir[1]. I wished Heathcliff would leave. He was like an evil beast, prowling around, waiting to spring and destroy us.

---

[1] heir – someone who is expected to inherit money or property

'Mr Heathcliff, be kind enough to bid this friend of yours release me – she forgets that you and I are not intimate acquaintances, and what amuses her is painful to me beyond expression.'

(Isabella to Heathcliff. Cathy is deliberately embarrassing her, Volume I, Chapter X)

One day, on the way to Wuthering Heights, I saw a child who looked just like Hindley Earnshaw as a boy. It turned out to be Hareton, swearing and cursing. Heathcliff had taught him to swear at his father.

The next time Heathcliff came to the house, I caught him embracing Miss Isabella. Later, in the kitchen, he and Miss Catherine had a terrible row. He accused her of treating him badly, and said he would have his revenge and marry Isabella. I fetched Edgar Linton, who followed me downstairs. They were still arguing, but stopped when he came in. Edgar told Heathcliff to leave immediately and to cease visiting Thrushcross Grange.

After more angry words, Heathcliff pushed the chair Edgar Linton was leaning on. Edgar hit him in the throat and walked out of the room. He returned with the gardeners and the coachman to seize Heathcliff, but Heathcliff left. Later, Edgar told Cathy she must choose between him and Heathcliff. Cathy became hysterical. She locked herself in her room and refused to eat.

Edgar told Isabella that if she encouraged Heathcliff, he would have nothing more to do with her.

'I wish you joy of the milk-blooded coward, Cathy!' said her friend. 'I compliment you on your taste: and that is the slavering, shivering thing you preferred to me! I would not strike him with my fist, but I'd kick him with my foot, and experience considerable satisfaction. Is he weeping, or is he going to faint for fear?'

(Heathcliff to Cathy, Volume I, Chapter XI)

On the third day, Catherine unbarred her door. She had convinced herself that Edgar did not love her and wanted her to die. She seemed to be sliding into madness. She told me that she longed to be out on the moors. And she longed for Heathcliff. She leaned out of the window in the cold winter night.

Hearing our voices, Edgar Linton hurried into the room. He was horrified to see his wife's condition. I decided to fetch the doctor. As I hurried to the road, I found Miss Isabella's dog, Fanny, tied with a handkerchief to a hook in the wall, half dead. I untied it and laid it in the garden.

Mr Kenneth, the doctor, came as soon as I told him Catherine was ill again. Desperately worried, I ran back to the house. Isabella's room was empty, but for the time being, I could say nothing. First, Mr Kenneth had to see Catherine. He was hopeful that she would recover, but she had to be kept quiet and calm.

Later, Isabella's absence was discovered. She had been seen the night before, riding away from the village – with Heathcliff. Edgar disowned[1] her.

---

[1] disowned – no longer recognised as a member of the family

'But, Heathcliff, if I dare you now, will you venture? If you do, I'll keep you. I'll not lie there by myself; they may bury me twelve feet deep, and throw the church down over me; but I won't rest till you are with me ... I never will!'

(Cathy, ranting, Volume I, Chapter XII)

The master nursed Catherine through what
Mr Kenneth said was a 'brain fever'[1]. Mr Kenneth
warned that Mrs Linton would be nothing but a
worry in the future.

In the spring, she at last left her bedroom and came
downstairs to sit in the parlour – she was expecting
a baby.

Six weeks after Heathcliff and Isabella left, we
received a note from Isabella, announcing their
marriage. Two weeks later, I received a long letter
from her. She had returned with Heathcliff to
Wuthering Heights – to Joseph and the drunken
Hindley.

Isabella was unhappy and longed for Thrushcross
Grange. How, she asked, having met Joseph and
Hindley, by now half-mad, was she to keep her own
sanity? Hareton had been taught no manners. On
her first evening at Wuthering Heights, Heathcliff
disappeared. She had no idea where to sleep. Joseph
had been his usual rude self. All she had to eat was a
bowl of porridge, which she preferred to eat alone.
Exhausted, she threw it on the floor, where the dog
immediately licked it up. She was miserable and
begged me to visit her.

---

[1] brain fever – delirium, madness

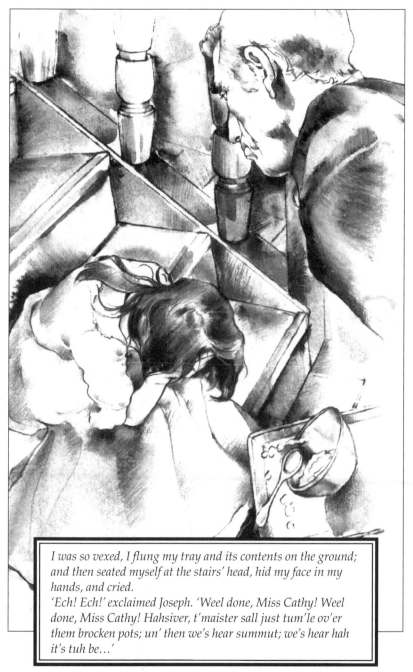

I was so vexed, I flung my tray and its contents on the ground; and then seated myself at the stairs' head, hid my face in my hands, and cried.

'Ech! Ech!' exclaimed Joseph. 'Weel done, Miss Cathy! Weel done, Miss Cathy! Hahsiver, t'maister sall just tum'le ov'er them brocken pots; un' then we's hear summut; we's hear hah it's tuh be…'

(Isabella, describing her first night at Wuthering Heights, Volume I, Chapter XIII)

As soon as I could, I visited Isabella at Wuthering Heights. She looked discouraged and slovenly. Heathcliff, by contrast, looked neat and gentlemanly. I warned him against trying to see Cathy again. I reminded him how ill she had been. Her life was calmer now.

He treated Isabella with contempt. In front of her, he spoke openly of his love for Cathy. He said that their meetings had made him realise how much they loved each other. Their feelings for each other were deeper than anyone else could possibly understand.

He ordered Isabella out of the room, then tried to persuade me to help him see Cathy. He argued and threatened until I could stand up to him no longer. I agreed to take a letter from him to Mrs Linton, and to let him know the next time Edgar Linton planned to be away from home. I, and the other servants, would also arrange to be out of the way. In view of his threats I had no choice…

*****

The doctor had arrived. Mrs Dean went downstairs to tell him I[1] was getting better. The rest of her story could wait until another day.

---

[1] Lockwood is narrating in this section

'My young lady is looking sadly the worse for her change of condition,' I remarked. 'Somebody's love comes short in her case, obviously – whose I may guess; but, perhaps, I shouldn't say.'

(Nelly, speaking to Heathcliff about Isabella, Volume I, Chapter XIV)

Volume Two

A week later, Nelly Dean continued her story…

*****

I waited three days until everyone went to church on Sunday then I gave Catherine Heathcliff's letter. I read the letter to her, and even as I read it Heathcliff came into the room and swept her into his arms. They kissed passionately.

Heathcliff could tell immediately that she was dying. His eyes were desperate. Catherine accused him of breaking her heart and said that he would not be sorry at her death. This drove him almost mad. He asked her how she could have married Edgar, knowing that she loved him, Heathcliff. She had brought this on herself, he said, but he would be left in hell. Now it was Catherine's turn to weep. Heathcliff held her as their tears flowed together.

Time was passing. I saw Mr Edgar come through the front gate. At last Heathcliff tried to leave. With shrieks and cries, Cathy begged him to stay. Edgar entered the room and threatened Heathcliff, but he picked up the now unconscious Cathy and told Edgar to help her at once. When she came round, her mind was gone. She recognised no one. Heathcliff said he would stay in the garden – all night, waiting.

'Why did you betray your own heart, Cathy? I have not one word of comfort – you deserve this. You have killed yourself. Yes, you may kiss me, and cry; and wring out my kisses and tears. They'll blight you – they'll damn you. You loved me – then what right had you to leave me?'

(Heathcliff to Cathy, Volume II, Chapter I)

That night, Catherine's baby was born – a girl. Two hours later, Catherine died. The baby was given her mother's name. Edgar was devastated. Exhausted, he laid his head on the pillow beside his wife, who wore an expression of perfect peace.

Later that morning I found Heathcliff in the garden, where he had spent the night. He was trembling, and I saw that he had feelings just as other men did. I told him that Catherine died quietly and peacefully. He exploded with rage and sorrow. He shouted that she should not rest in peace while he was still alive. She had left him alone – to suffer.

Catherine's coffin lay in the drawing room, surrounded by flowers. Edgar stayed with her day and night. Heathcliff remained in the garden. When Edgar went to get some rest, I let Heathcliff in one last time. He put a lock of his hair in a locket that she wore. Finding one of her curls on the floor, I twisted it with his and closed the locket on them both.

Catherine was buried on a green slope in a corner of the churchyard. Eventually, Edgar was buried beside her, but that was years later…

'Catherine Earnshaw, may you not rest, as long as I am living! You said I killed you – haunt me, then! The murdered do haunt their murderers. I believe – I know that ghosts have wandered on Earth. Be with me always – take any form – drive me mad! Only do not leave me in this abyss, where I cannot find you! Oh, God! It is unutterable! I cannot live without my life! I cannot live without my soul!'

(Heathcliff, Volume II, Chapter II)

The next day, I was looking after the baby girl when Isabella, Mrs Heathcliff, arrived, breathless and soaking wet, with a deep cut under one ear. She took off her wedding ring, smashed it with the poker and threw it into the fire. She had left Heathcliff.

There had been terrible scenes at Wuthering Heights. Hindley had threatened Heathcliff with a gun. Heathcliff overpowered the drunken Hindley and kicked him as he lay on the floor. Isabella had told Heathcliff that if he and Catherine had married, she too would have grown to hate him. Enraged, he threw a kitchen knife at her, giving her a deep cut. She had run away, never to return.

Isabella went to the south, near London, where some months later she had a son whom she named Linton. I knew this because she and Edgar began to write to each other again.

Six months later, Hindley died. He was only twenty-seven years old. Hindley had mortgaged[1] everything he owned to Heathcliff to pay for his alcohol and gambling. Heathcliff was now the owner of Wuthering Heights, and Hareton was in his care. Heathcliff planned to bring up Hareton in his own ways, as a further revenge on the Earnshaws.

---

[1] mortgaged – obtained a loan against the value of property. If repayments are not met, the property can be seized.

'… instead of endeavouring to reach me, he snatched a dinner knife from the table, and flung it at my head. It struck beneath my ear, and stopped the sentence I was uttering; but pulling it out, I sprang to the door…'

(Isabella telling Nelly Dean about Heathcliff throwing a knife at her, Volume II, Chapter III)

Young Catherine grew into a beautiful girl. Edgar taught her himself and she learned quickly and eagerly. He made sure she stayed safely inside the grounds of Thrushcross Grange. When Catherine was twelve years old, Edgar had to go to see his sister, Isabella. She was ill and not recovering. Edgar was away for three weeks.

One day, I found Miss Cathy at Wuthering Heights, laughing and chatting to Hareton, now a big, strong lad of eighteen. When she realised that Hareton was not Heathcliff's son, her manner changed and she spoke to him as if he were a servant. This made him very angry. He began to curse and use bad language. Miss Cathy had never heard such language before. She ordered Hareton, then the serving woman, to bring her pony. They refused. Cathy began to weep and threw herself into my arms. At last we managed to leave. Hareton seemed sorry to have upset her, and tried to give her one of his puppies.

On the way home, I explained that her father did not like the people at Wuthering Heights. If he found out that she had gone there while I was in charge, I might lose my job. Catherine promised that it would be our secret.

'What's the matter? Get my horse, I say.'
'I'll see thee damned, before I be thy servant!' growled the lad.
'You'll see me what?' asked Catherine in surprise.
'Damned – thou saucy witch!' he replied.

(Young Catherine and Hareton, Volume II, Chapter IV)

Isabella died, and Edgar returned from his journey with Linton Heathcliff, the son of Isabella and Heathcliff. The boy was just six months younger than Miss Cathy.

Cathy was wild with excitement and could not wait to meet Linton. He turned out to be a very delicate child, still weeping for his mother. Cathy was gentle and patient with him.

I worried about what would happen to the boy if he were taken to live at Wuthering Heights with his father and Hareton.

That night, Joseph appeared and demanded the child. Edgar told him that Linton was asleep and could not possibly travel to Wuthering Heights that night. As Joseph left without the boy, he shouted that Heathcliff would come himself in the morning.

'Oh, he'll do very well,' said the master to me, after watching them a minute. 'Very well, if we can keep him, Ellen. The company of a child of his own age will instill new spirit into him soon: and by wishing for strength he'll gain it.'
'Aye, if we can keep him!' I mused to myself; and sore misgivings came over me that there was slight hope of that.

(Edgar and Nelly, Volume II, Chapter V)

Early the next day, Mr Edgar told me to take his nephew to Wuthering Heights. Young Linton did not want to go, and was puzzled that he was to meet his father. Isabella had never mentioned Heathcliff.

I told him that Isabella had lived in the south of England for her health. Heathcliff stayed in the north for his work. I tried to put everything in a good light. The boy was so small and weak.

When Heathcliff saw his son, he made no secret of his disappointment, calling him a 'puling[1] chicken', and saying that his mother was a slut. He soon realised that the boy needed a lot of care. When Edgar died, young Linton, through his mother, would inherit Thrushcross Grange[2]. Heathcliff's son would then have the two biggest houses in the neighbourhood. I was glad that Heathcliff had reason to make sure that Linton regained his health. Hareton, Joseph and the other servants were to treat him as the young master. Heathcliff planned to bring him up as a gentleman with a good education.

As I left, I was sad to hear Linton crying aloud, begging to come with me.

[1] puling – crying or whining
[2] the nearest male heir inherited property. Linton came before Cathy, even though she was Edgar's daughter and was older than Linton.

'God! what a beauty! What a lovely, charming thing!' he exclaimed. 'Haven't they reared it on snails, and sour milk, Nelly? Oh, damn my soul, but that's worse than I expected – and the devil knows I was not sanguine.'

(Heathcliff, speaking about his son, Linton, Volume II, Chapter VI)

Mr Edgar did not want Miss Cathy to know that Linton was at Wuthering Heights, so we kept it from her.

Four years later, on Cathy's sixteenth birthday, we met Heathcliff and Hareton on the moor. Heathcliff invited us to Wuthering Heights and Cathy insisted that we go. Cathy and Linton were delighted to see each other. She couldn't understand why she hadn't been told that he was at Wuthering Heights. Linton was very tired and wanted only to sit by the fire, so Cathy walked in the garden with Hareton.

Heathcliff said he was proud of the way he had brought up Hareton – working him hard, giving him no education. It was part of his revenge on Hindley, who had treated him the same way. He was charming to Cathy, and lied about Edgar's reasons for keeping her away. Cathy blamed her father and me for not telling her where Linton was. She didn't realise that Heathcliff was hiding his real nature. Edgar warned her about Heathcliff and described his cruel treatment of Isabella, her aunt.

Later, I learned that Cathy had begun writing to young Linton. I made her burn the letters. I also sent a message to Linton, telling him to write no more.

'What, Linton!' cried Cathy, kindling into joyful surprise at the name. 'Is that little Linton? He's taller than I am! Are you Linton?'
The youth stepped forward, and acknowledged himself: she kissed him fervently, and they gazed with wonder at the change time had wrought in the appearance of each.

(Cathy and Linton meeting, Volume II, Chapter VII)

With the ending of her little romance, which had
hardly begun, Cathy became sad and quiet.
Mr Edgar caught a bad cold that lasted all winter
and had to stay indoors.

One day, Cathy and I were out walking. She climbed
the wall of the estate to get some rose hips and her hat
fell off, over the other side of the wall. She climbed
down to get it but could not get back. To my horror,
Heathcliff came riding by and began to talk to her.
He said that young Linton was dying of a broken
heart. He would be dead by the summer unless she
went to his rescue.

I shouted to Heathcliff to stop telling lies. He had not
realised I was there, but he repeated that Linton was
dying. I finally got a nearby door open and went out
to get Cathy. Heathcliff said that he would be away
all week and again begged her to see Linton.

At home, Cathy could not stop weeping. The next
day, against my better judgment, I accompanied her
to Wuthering Heights. Perhaps Linton would not be
as ill as Heathcliff claimed; perhaps he would not be
pleased to see Cathy. I could only hope.

'Miss Catherine, I'll own to you that I have little patience with Linton – and Hareton and Joseph have less. I'll own that he's with a harsh set. He pines for kindness, as well as love; and a kind word from you would be his best medicine.'

(Heathcliff to Cathy, Volume II, Chapter VIII)

Catherine rode her pony to Wuthering Heights while I walked beside her. My feet got soaking wet. When we reached the farmhouse, Cathy and I went in to see Linton. He was slumped in a large chair, fretful and complaining. He and Cathy got into a violent argument about their parents. He told Cathy that her mother hated her father and loved his father, Heathcliff. Cathy was so upset that she gave his chair a hard shove, causing him to have a long fit of coughing.

I became worried, but at last it ended. Cathy felt sorry for Linton again and made a fuss over him, trying to make him comfortable, which was not easy. We stayed for a long time. When we left she seemed determined to see him again.

I thought he was a dreadful boy, and not long for this world. I had to find a way to prevent Cathy from seeing him again. Unfortunately, I fell ill the next day from sitting so long at Wuthering Heights in wet clothes. For three weeks, Catherine looked after me wonderfully well. Between Mr Edgar and myself, she had no time for meals or studies, or play.
Only in the evenings, she had a little time for herself.

'Well, I'll tell you something!' said Linton. 'Your mother hated your father, now then.'
'Oh!' exclaimed Catherine, too enraged to continue.
'And she loved mine!' added he.
'You little liar! I hate you now,' she panted, and her face grew red with passion.

(Cathy and Linton, Volume II, Chapter IX)

After three weeks, I was able to get up and spend the evenings with Cathy. I discovered that during my illness she had been going out on her pony to Wuthering Heights.

One night, she told me, Hareton showed her how he could read his name over the door. He was very proud of this, but Cathy had laughed because he couldn't read the numbers. I interrupted her when I heard this. Hareton deserved her respect for trying to learn. She had been very rude to him.

Sometimes, Catherine and Linton got on well together. Mostly they had arguments that were started by Linton. Catherine gradually realised that he would never be happy, nor would he allow those around him to be happy, either. Nevertheless, she was pleased that she was learning to put up with his self-pitying ways.

I was very worried and told her father about her secret visits. Mr Edgar was shocked and unhappy. He wrote to young Linton to tell him that Catherine would not be going to Wuthering Heights again. If he wished to see her, he must come to the Grange.

'Miss Catherine! I can read yon, nah.'
'Wonderful,' I exclaimed. 'Pray, let us hear you – you are
grown clever!'
He spelt and drawled over by syllables, the name –
'Hareton Earnshaw.'
'And the figures?' I cried, encouragingly, perceiving that he
came to a dead halt.
'I cannot tell them yet,' he answered.
'Oh, you dunce!' I said, laughing heartily at his failure.

(Catherine, telling Nelly about Hareton's reading, Volume II, Chapter X)

55

Mr Edgar was very worried about what Cathy would do after his death. As he grew weaker, he began to think about his daughter's future. He often told me his thoughts. He wondered if young Linton would be able to take his place, and invited him to visit the Grange. Linton wrote that Heathcliff would not allow him to, but offered to meet somewhere else. At last, Mr Edgar agreed that Cathy and Linton could walk or ride together once a week under my supervision.

It was late summer when Catherine and I set out to meet Linton. We finally reached him only a quarter of a mile from Wuthering Heights. He was lying on the heath looking very weak indeed.

Catherine tried hard to amuse him, but he showed little interest. Cathy thought because he was too weak to complain as he had done before, that he must be getting better. To me, he appeared much, much worse. He was clearly terrified of appearing weak or of being too quiet. He was also terrified of his father and kept looking around to see if he was coming.

He lay on the heath, awaiting our approach, and did not rise till we came within a few yards. Then, he walked so feebly, and looked so pale, that I immediately exclaimed, 'Why, Master Heathcliff, you are not fit for enjoying a ramble this morning. How ill you do look!'

(Nelly describing meeting young Linton Heathcliff, Volume II, Chapter XII)

A week later, we met young Linton at the same place. He was as weak as before. When Heathcliff appeared, he lay on the ground, clinging to Cathy. Heathcliff asked her to help Linton walk back to Wuthering Heights. Cathy could not refuse.

As soon as we entered the house, Heathcliff shut the door and locked it. Cathy tried to fight him for the key but he hit her cruelly about the head. Linton, who had been used as a decoy to get us there, told us Heathcliff's plan. He and Catherine were to be married the next morning. I told him that he was no fit husband for my beautiful Catherine.

Heathcliff returned. Though Catherine begged and pleaded, Heathcliff seemed to enjoy her unhappiness. On her knees, she begged him to let her go. Heathcliff's response was to call her a snake and threaten to kick her.

Catherine and I spent the night upstairs in Zillah's room, where we were awake all night.

At seven o'clock, Heathcliff took Cathy away, leaving me alone for the next five nights. Hareton brought food only once a day and he did not speak.

'Have you never loved anybody, in all your life, uncle? Never? Ah! you must look once – I'm so wretched – you can't help being sorry and pitying me.'
'Keep your eft's [small, lizard-like animal] fingers off; and move, or I'll kick you!' cried Heathcliff, brutally repulsing her.

(Cathy and Heathcliff, Volume II, Chapter XIII)

Zillah finally returned five mornings later. She was surprised to see me. Everyone thought I was dead. Mr Edgar, she told me, was not dead but was expected to last no more than a day.

Linton told me that Cathy, now his wife, was locked upstairs. At one point, in an argument about a necklace, Heathcliff had knocked her to the ground. How could Linton just watch while she was treated so badly? Heathcliff was outside. I hurriedly left and returned to Thrushcross Grange. Servants from the Grange would be sent to rescue Cathy later.

Mr Edgar was even more ill than when I had last seen him. I told him how we had been held at Wuthering Heights and about Cathy's marriage. I did not mention the violence. At last young Linton helped Cathy to escape. She was able to be with her father during his last moments. He was weak, ill, but radiantly happy to have his daughter at his bedside.

No sooner had he died, than Mr Green, Heathcliff's solicitor, appeared and dismissed all the servants except myself. Cathy, now Mrs Linton Heathcliff, was to return to Wuthering Heights immediately after her father's funeral.

He died blissfully, Mr Lockwood; he died so.
Kissing her cheek he murmured, 'I am going to her, and you,
darling child, shall come to us,' and never stirred or spoke
again, but continued that rapt, radiant gaze, till his pulse
imperceptibly stopped, and his soul departed.

(Nelly describing Mr Edgar's death, Volume II, Chapter XIV)

Heathcliff came to order Cathy back to Wuthering Heights. He had punished Linton for helping her escape. Linton, he said, blamed her for his punishment and would treat her worse than he had before. Cathy replied that at least she and Linton loved each other. There was no one to love Heathcliff.

While she was getting her things, Heathcliff told me a sad and horrible tale. After the funeral, the sexton was digging Edgar Linton's grave. Heathcliff made him uncover Catherine's coffin, and he looked inside. Her face was still recognisable[1]. He loosened the side of the coffin, the side away from Linton's grave. He planned to be buried beside her. He paid the sexton to remove the side panels from his own coffin so that he and Catherine could be together, at last.

Heathcliff said that for the last eighteen years he had been haunted by Catherine's spirit. He was sure he could feel her, always near him but just out of sight. Now, having seen the dead Catherine and made his arrangements, he felt more peaceful. Forbidding me to visit my darling Cathy, he took the poor girl away.

[1] Medically, this is quite possible. The weather had turned cold at the time of Catherine's burial, which would have helped to preserve the body.

'I'll tell you what I did yesterday! I got the sexton, who was digging Linton's grave, to remove the earth off her coffin lid, and I opened it. I thought, once, I would have stayed there, when I saw her face again – it is hers yet – he had hard work to stir me; but he said it would change, if the air blew on it ...'

(Heathcliff, Volume II, Chapter XV)

Now, my only news of Cathy came from Zillah.
When Cathy returned to Wuthering Heights, Linton
was dying. He never left his room again. Cathy had
no rest. Zillah sometimes saw her crying, at the top
of the stairs. But Zillah had orders from Heathcliff
not to interfere or even help.

Linton died, leaving all of his, and Cathy's, property
to Heathcliff. Cathy was penniless. Some land still
belonged to her, but she was completely under
Heathcliff's control. When at last she came
downstairs, Hareton tried to be friendly. He tidied
himself up and tried to take an interest in Cathy's
books. She was cold and haughty towards him.

I thought about using my savings to buy a cottage
and take Cathy to live with me, but I knew that
Heathcliff would never allow it. Her only other
chance would be to marry again, but that is beyond
my power to bring about…

*****

So ended Mrs Dean's story. I, Lockwood, was getting
over my illness and planned to spend six months in
London, ending my tenancy of Thrushcross Grange
in October. I could not face another winter in the
neighbourhood of Wuthering Heights.

… *he put out his hand and stroked one curl, as gently as if it were a bird. He might have stuck a knife into her neck, she started round in such a taking.*
'Get away, this moment! How dare you touch me? Why are you stopping there?' she cried, in a tone of disgust.

(Hareton and Cathy, Volume II, Chapter XIV)

The next morning I[1] went to Wuthering Heights to give notice of my decision. Mr Heathcliff was not expected home until dinner time. As I waited for him, Hareton Earnshaw came in – to keep an eye on me, I thought.

Catherine was helping to prepare vegetables for the meal. She was sulky, and quieter than before. I thought she was very beautiful but, from Mrs Dean's descriptions, not of good character. Cathy told me that she had no writing materials, and that Heathcliff had destroyed her books. Hareton had a few books and sometimes tried to teach himself to read but Catherine laughed at his mistakes. Hareton brought Catherine his books, but again she refused them and made fun of him. He could stand it no longer and hit her in the mouth; then, hurt and angry, he threw the books on the fire.

Heathcliff returned and I told him of my changed plans. He looked thinner than before. Catherine was sent to the kitchen to eat with Joseph. I had a dreary meal with Heathcliff and Hareton, and did not see Catherine before I left.

I rode away, thinking how Catherine's life would have changed had she and I fallen in love. That was what Nelly Dean had hoped.

---

[1] Mr Lockwood has taken up the story again.

[Hareton's] *endeavours to raise himself had produced just the contrary result.*
'*Yes, that's all the good such a brute as you can get from them!*' *cried Catherine, sucking her damaged lip, and watching the conflagration with indignant eyes.*
'*You'd better hold your tongue, now!*' *he answered fiercely.*

(Volume II, Chapter XVIII)

In September I returned unexpectedly to Thrushcross Grange. I was told that Nelly Dean was at Wuthering Heights. I went to find her. The doors and windows were open, and a coal fire glowed from within. Inside were two figures: Hareton and Cathy. They were clearly in love. Catherine looked so beautiful that I regretted not having fallen in love with her myself.

I went round to the kitchen and there found – Nelly Dean. She had taken the place of Zillah, who had left. Most surprising of all, Heathcliff was dead. Nelly told the story in her own way…

*****

I[1] returned to Wuthering Heights within two weeks of your leaving us, Mr Lockwood. I was pleased to be able to make life a little more comfortable for Catherine.

One day, Cathy tried to make friends with Hareton again. He was afraid of her teasing, and spoke harshly to her. Cathy wept that he hated her – as much as Heathcliff did. Hareton replied that he had angered Heathcliff many times by taking her part. Cathy begged his forgiveness and gave him a gentle kiss on the cheek. She wrapped one of her nicest books as a gift for him. He accepted it and the two sat happily together.

[1] Nelly Dean.

'... it was lucky he could not see her face, or he would never
have been so steady – I could, and I bit my lip, in spite, at having
thrown away the chance I might have had, of doing something
besides staring at its smiting beauty.'

(Lockwood, observing Catherine and Hareton, Volume II, Chapter XVIII)

The next morning, Hareton cleared some of Joseph's blackcurrant trees because Cathy wanted flowerbeds instead. Joseph was upset and threatened to leave. Heathcliff turned on Hareton, but Cathy spoke up. She accused Heathcliff of taking her land and her money, and said that Hareton would not allow him to hurt her. Heathcliff called her a witch and grabbed her by the hair to hit her. Suddenly, he looked into her face and let her go.

Now, Catherine and Hareton helped each other. Hareton learned quickly from Catherine. The more she praised him, the harder he worked.

Heathcliff, coming home unexpectedly one evening, found us all three together. He could see at a glance how things were between Cathy and Hareton. He sent them from the room and spoke to me alone. Both Cathy and Hareton resembled his Catherine, he said. Cathy was her daughter, Hareton her nephew. Every time he looked at them, he felt again the agony of losing her.

All these years, he had worked for revenge on the Lintons and the Earnshaws. Now his revenge was almost complete, but he was losing interest. He was losing interest in life.

He had his hand in her hair; Hareton attempted to release the locks, entreating him not to hurt her that once. His black eyes flashed, he seemed ready to tear Catherine in pieces ... of a sudden, his fingers relaxed, he shifted his grasp from her head, to her arm, and gazed intently in her face...

(Volume II, Chapter XIX)

After our conversation, Heathcliff kept even more to himself. One night, I heard him go out. By morning he had still not returned. He came back after breakfast, pale and trembling, and his eyes glittered strangely.

Later, he walked up and down the garden. When he came in, he appeared strangely happy, but pale and tense. For the next three days, he refused to eat. He became so thin, he began to look like a goblin and I was terrified of going in to his room.

Then, early one morning, he reminded me how he wished to be buried, next to his Catherine. That night, he locked himself in his room. As I walked in the garden the following morning, I saw his window swinging open with the rain driving in. Going to his room, I opened the panels of the bed. He was dead. Only Hareton wept for him.

Mr Kenneth, the doctor, was puzzled about how Heathcliff died. I didn't mention that he hadn't eaten for days. It might have caused trouble for us all.

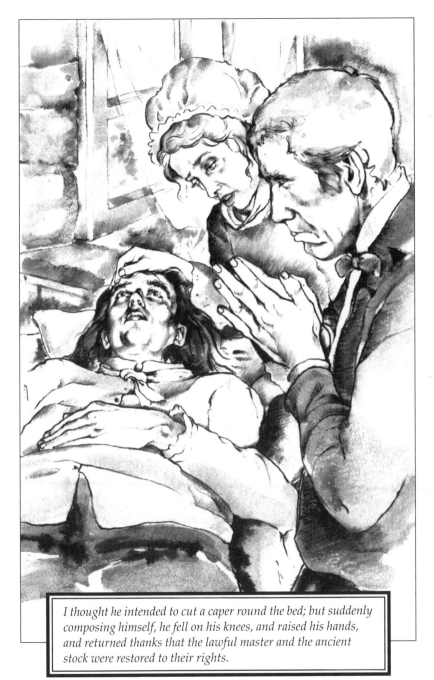

I thought he intended to cut a caper round the bed; but suddenly composing himself, he fell on his knees, and raised his hands, and returned thanks that the lawful master and the ancient stock were restored to their rights.

(Nelly describes Joseph praying for his master, Volume II, Chapter XX)

Heathcliff was buried next to Catherine, according to his instructions. Earnshaw and I, the sexton and the six men who carried the coffin all saw the proceedings. The news spread through the neighbourhood and people were shocked. Later, there were stories of people seeing Heathcliff's ghost – near the church, on the moor, and at Wuthering Heights…

*****

Mrs Dean's story[1] had come to an end. Hareton and Catherine were to live at Thrushcross Grange after their marriage on New Year's Day. Nelly was looking forward to being their housekeeper.

Only old Joseph, with perhaps a youth to keep him company, would stay on at Wuthering Heights. They would live in the kitchen with the rest of the house shut.

I said goodbye to Nelly Dean and Joseph, and walked back to the Grange by way of the church. There were the three headstones on the slope next to the moor: belonging to Edgar Linton, Catherine Linton and Heathcliff. The place was so calm and beautiful, I was sure that they slept peacefully in that quiet earth.

[1] Lockwood resumes the tale.

I lingered round them, under that benign sky; watched the moths fluttering among the heath, and hare-bells; listened to the soft wind breathing through the grass; and wondered how any one could ever imagine unquiet slumbers, for the sleepers in that quiet earth.

(Volume II, Chapter XX)

*Also available in the
Graphic Novels Series:*

GREAT EXPECTATIONS
CHARLES DICKENS

THE MAYOR OF CASTERBRIDGE
THOMAS HARDY

PRIDE AND PREJUDICE
JANE AUSTEN

Retold by Hilary Burningham

See over for details of our Graphic Shakespeare Series

*If you enjoyed reading this book,
you may wish to read other books in the
sister series:*

The Graphic Shakespeare Series

The titles in the Graphic Shakespeare Series
are an ideal introduction to Shakespeare's
plays, but can equally well be used
as revision aids.

The main characters and key events
are brought to life in the simplified story
and dramatic pictures, and the short extracts
from the original play focus on key speeches
in Shakespeare's language.

Available in the
Graphic Shakespeare Series:

A Midsummer Night's Dream
Henry V
Julius Caesar
Macbeth
Romeo and Juliet
The Tempest
Twelfth Night

EVANS BROTHERS LIMITED